Heroin

Jesus

Heroin
Jesus

Danny Cosby

TATE PUBLISHING
AND ENTERPRISES, LLC

Published by Tate Publishing & Enterprises, LLC
127 E. Trade Center Terrace | Mustang, Oklahoma 73064 USA
1.888.361.9473 | www.tatepublishing.com

Tate Publishing is committed to excellence in the publishing industry. The company reflects the philosophy established by the founders, based on Psalm 68:11,
"The Lord gave the word and great was the company of those who published it."

Book design copyright © 2014 by Tate Publishing, LLC. All rights reserved.
Cover design by Junriel Boquecosa
Interior design by Jimmy Sevilleno

Published in the United States of America

ISBN: 978-1-63418-391-8
Biography & Autobiography / Personal Memoirs
14.10.15

After much thought and prayer I've decided to
dedicate this book to the guy who was preaching
at the homeless shelter on September 18, 2005.
I don't know what your name is, but God used you to
pierce through my soul and make a lasting change.
From the bottom of my heart, thank
you for being there that night

Contents

Foreword

SOME THINGS DON'T make sense...

It's funny and fascinating to me how God works. He loves to whisper things too often in my ears that on this side of heaven don't make sense. Those of us who live our lives for God are guided by that "still small voice," that unction in our gut, or unusual thought that we know we are supposed to do something that is out of our ordinary line of reason or behavior.

I'm the director of worship at a large church in Tennessee. Before I took this job in January of 2000, I had been a traveling singer-songwriter, making records and performing concerts all over the world. I still do that, just much less often. God had blessed me with industry recognition and success. I've won a couple of Grammys and some Dove Awards (the gospel equivalent of the Grammy), and I've sold around some three million records. I assure you, it didn't make sense when God told me to become a full-time, on-staff worship leader, but I did—and it's changed my life and the lives of my family in a wonderful way!

So, when God brought Danny Cosby to me, it was another case where God was telling me to do something that didn't make sense on several levels. I didn't really need another tenor on my front line at the time, and Danny didn't really play an instrument well enough to sit in with the worship team. But I told him he could jump in the choir and possibly sing a special if he was good enough and if he "checked out." (It's a good idea to at least do a minimum investigation into a person's character before you put them on a platform). I didn't have to dig too far to discover Danny had been in trouble and done prison time for non-violent crimes. Danny was very open about sharing his past. Even so, I kept feeling like I was supposed to go down this road with Danny. I was hesitant to move too fast with him, but God kept moving me to give him all the privileges I had available. God kept reminding me that Danny was a forgiven man who needed another chance—Just like He told other people to do for me, once upon a time.

I don't even remember when I first heard Danny sing, but I remember I loved his voice. It had gravel in it, and he sang like a redeemed man—it takes one to know one! He projected the confidence of a man who knew his gifting and, at the same time, a brokenness that comes from a man who knows God's undeserved favor. I was aware that there were other churches and people who were unwilling to give Danny a chance because of his past. I can't say they were wrong for doing that—maybe Danny wasn't ready. I'm learning not to judge what others in leadership do. All I know is God was telling *me* to give Danny another chance. So I said, "Okay, Lord." That was four-and-a-half years ago. I have never regretted it.

I've often thought about what I could have messed up by not doing what didn't make sense, all the people who would have missed out on being blessed by hearing Danny sing or give his testimony. Maybe he wouldn't have met his future bride and the love of his life, Johanna (who worked for me and was working for the church when Danny arrived), and wouldn't have become the daddy and role model her son, Christopher, needed so desperately.

At the end of the day, God did all of it. I'm glad he let me be the vessel. He spoke through to say, "Yes, it's time" to Danny. I'm happy to be able to call Danny my friend and brother in Christ. My life is better for having met him. Our worship team and church body is better off with Danny as part of it. Danny's journeys is worth reading about and, as you read this book, remember that God often directs us to do things that don't seem to make sense at the time, only to realize that what He was asking of us made perfect sense all along.

—Bruce Carroll,
Worship Leader / Singer-Songwriter /
Grammy and Dove Award-winning artist

Introduction

WHY THE TITLE *Heroin Jesus* you ask? Well, for starters my little brother came up with the name as I was talking with him about actually writing the book. He knows about my past addiction to heroin and many other drugs, and how it was an encounter in a homeless shelter with Jesus through a preacher in this homeless shelter that radically changed the direction my life was heading. After making the decision to write this book, I began to pray and ask God what this title really meant, and he showed me in his Word the comparison to the title. In Revelations chapter 3 verse 20, the Bible says actually Jesus says to John who is writing this particular book on an island he was exiled to called Patmos because they could not kill him no matter how they tried he had the protective hand of the Lord upon his life and so they decided to throw him on an island that was comprised mostly of rock and no vegetation believing he would probably starve to death but it was here that Jesus met with him to write this amazing book properly named revelation the last book of the Bible. Once John had gotten through the first two chapters (as we have chaptered them later on in time but to him it was probably just one steady stream of writing, verse 20 says), Jesus said, behold I stand at the door, and knock, if any man opens I will come in and sup with him and he with me.

Now on the surface, you might say, "What does that have to do with anything?" Well, let me explain to you how that has something to do with everything. In my particular addiction, I moved from taking drugs orally to intravenously, and after looking back and thinking on the different times that I would self-medicate, I realized that the moment or moments before I would take the drugs, Jesus was knocking on the door of my heart and every time I would self medicate I would go numb and quiet the knock of his hand on the door of my heart. However, Jesus is not like us in that we give up after a certain amount of attempts at getting someone's attention; He is relentless in his pursuit of us—so relentless that many, many years ago, He left his throne in heaven, laid aside all of his glory and power to come to earth as a baby, and grow up as a normal human being but without sin He was nailed to a piece of wood as the perfect sacrifice for all the sins of the world past, present, and future. Now I know I just dropped a bomb on you right there if by chance you have not already come to have faith in Jesus, but that's okay because it's meant to be overwhelming; it's also meant to be simple. The Bible says that you are saved from your sins and from an eternity in hell by the grace of Jesus Christ, and that it is a gift from him to you, not something you work for to earn. This is what the Bible means by saying that for some people, Jesus is a stumbling block and not a stepping stone. The older we get, the more we want to be able to explain away everything in detail. We just simply don't believe that we can be given a gift and that something so profound as eternal life can be given to us just by simply believing that Jesus died in our place. But that's okay; whether you believe it or not, it is still the truth. Just because I don't play piano, that doesn't mean other people can't play the piano as well. It just means they're better at playing the piano than I am since it is an instrument that can and should be played. That might be not the greatest example, but I think you get the point.

Well, to wrap this all up, this introduction is my way of saying first and foremost, thank you for taking the time to pick this book up, but also it is my hope and prayer that this will lead you into a deeper, more intimate relationship with Jesus. You may have given your life to him at a young age and walked away, or you may have never given your life to him and you're wondering why in the world you're even reading this right now. Either way, I can tell you this much: nothing happens by chance. I have learned that every moment in your life, even the small, mundane, things, are monumental moments appointed by God. Jesus, in John chapter 17, prayed a prayer for his disciples at that time and also for us; and his words around verse 3 of that chapter have echoed from that moment he prayed it all the way through the hallways of time to right now, and what he said in that verse was this—and it is a prayer request from Jesus to God the Father. He said, I pray that they will know you the only true God and Jesus Christ whom you have sent and this is eternal life. Did you hear that? We all want to know about eternity and where we are going and what will happen when we get there, and Jesus gives us the answer right there! He said the word *know*. Bottom line, Jesus wants a relationship with you; he wants you to know that to him you are priceless even if other people have said you are worthless. The Bible says that the whole world can be against me as long as God is for me, and I'm writing to tell you today that no matter how bad you messed up, no matter how many bridges you burned, God is for you! You are not alone, and if you think God could not love you or forgive you, then keep on reading and hopefully by the end of this book—which is simply my story—you can say with me and many others God does love me! He never left me; I'm the one who left him! Jesus, I want to know you more intimately! Well, I appreciate you for taking the time to read this because in Revelation 12 there's a verse that says we are made "overcomers" by the blood of the Lamb and the word of our testimony. This is my testimony, on how I realized that the drugs were my way of trying to get away from God, and how I eventually accepted what Jesus was offering me, and how I am now enjoying life to the fullest. Not every day is all roses; I have a lot of bad days, but my good days definitely outweigh my bad ones now! I also pray that this book will stir up a desire for you to tell your story because your story will reach someone mine never will. The devil wants one thing from us, and that's our joy which brings us victory, usually because we have been telling people about how Jesus set us free. Therefore, I desire and hope that this book will cause many of you to want to begin telling your story or to write a book just like this. Grace and peace to you!

A Family Rescued

"If my people, who are called by my name,
will humble themselves and pray and seek
my face and turn from their wicked ways,
then will I hear from heaven and will forgive
their sin and will heal their land."

—2 Chronicles 7:14 (KJV)

YEP, I WAS the son of a preacher. I was the firstborn of Danny and Glenda Cosby, a couple who had met under quite trying circumstances. Both my parents had come from abusive and broken homes. My dad suffered extreme physical and verbal abuse at the hands of his father. Being the youngest of four boys and having a younger sister, it didn't help his mental state to have lost a brother to a car accident at a young age as well. My dad turned to drugs at a young age, as what would seem to be a natural move from years of beatings and verbal abuse, and at about twenty years of age, he met my mother. My mother, who lost both parents to heart attacks, found herself being raised by her alcoholic brother, and at about age fourteen, she was pretty much in the streets. She tells me a story about how she wore the same pair of jeans every day for one school year, and how for about three days of one week in particular she lived off a can of green beans and some bread until a high school friend let her stay over one night, and she ate a good meal. My parents may not be the focus of this book, but their triumphant story of rising out of the ashes to find one another and then ultimately finding Christ together, I believe, is the basis and foundation on which I find myself writing this book. Therefore, I find it necessary to briefly share their journey. My mother was eighteen when she met my dad, and after many ups and downs in dating, these two broken and wounded people found themselves sitting in an old brick church in Frayser, Tennessee, one Sunday. My mother tells me that my dad wanted to go, that he "needed to change his life," and she said that she went to make fun of him because she had "heard all that God-stuff before." Well, as you have heard it said, "The Lord works in mysterious ways," My mom and dad gave their life to Jesus that day, and not too much longer they were married and a loudmouthed baby named Danny Lee Cosby Jr. entered the world. I am so grateful that they turned their lives over to Jesus, because if they had not, I don't know what might have happened to them or us as a family. I've heard it said that the longer you wait and the older you get, the more callous your heart gets toward the pin pricks of the Gospel of Jesus on your heart. I'm so glad they responded to the "pricks" at a young time in their life; I know that I am still reaping the benefits from growing in the womb of a praying woman. Even now as I write this, I realize the importance of yielding myself on a daily basis to the Lord because it's really not about me, but those who are looking to me to be an example of Christ to them. Let us put everything aside that would hinder us and run this race called life with everything we've got to bring our loved ones safely into the arms of heaven's darling son, Jesus. Well, I didn't mean to get on a soapbox there, so back to the story.

I spent about the first ten years of my life in that little ol' brick church with its ol' wooden pews and hymnals. Yep, that's right. No big screens with lyrics on it, just an ol' book, an ol' piano, and two hands to clap. Ah, but those were some fun times as I remember those twenty to thirty people shouting songs of praise. I remember such a closeness among that small group of people, such big love in a small place. I remember dinners after service and Easter egg hunts. However, as a child, you see with eyes untainted by jealousy, greed, and lust; and as an adult, now I believe that I now know why some people may have wandered away from one another. There were great memories though. Sometimes it was a little scary watching a lady kick off her shoes and take off running in circles, shouting in what seemed to be a language I had never heard before, but looking back now God has showed a lot from what I experienced in that little ol' church in Frayser, Tennessee.

Within those ten years, my parents had two more kids, my sister Bonnie and brother Joshua, and around about when I was 8 or 9, the church asked my dad to be the new pastor. He gladly took on the job as he had always been as passionate about Jesus after his conversion as he was about scoring dope before Jesus entered his life; and many years later, I would find myself doing the same thing. It's amazing to me, how God is able to rescue one generation after another when they call on His name. Well, after a few years of preaching, my dad came home one day and told us we wouldn't be going back to that church. Later on I found out about something called legalism, which put a bad taste in my dad's mouth and caused him to run away from the church in general; but God in all His wisdom brought my dad back and we followed.

I remember being about twelve years old when we went to this huge building they called Bellevue Baptist, and it seemed like there was no end to the hallways or activities in this giant place. It was there that I began singing in the kids' choir, and one day a sweet lady approached me and said, "Young man, walk with me to this piano." It was at that piano that God made me the "O Holy Night" sing-ing Christmas tree kid for the next two years. I remem-ber standing there, holding the microphone and seeing the thousands of people, but as quickly as I felt frightened, I remember feeling a calm at twelve years of age on that stage, as if the Lord put his hand on my shoulder and said, "Sing, son. Sing." I spent most of my teen years at Bellevue in plays and singing for Sunday school classes. Ah, but at about sixteen years of age, I had already lost my virgin-ity and was well on my way to anything and everything that had nothing to do with God. I didn't realize it then, but God was with me through it all, like the patient vocal instructor who hears the student's voice cracking during a warm-up but knows there is a glorious reward of a beauti-ful song at the end of the rehearsal and confidence for the singer to boot. I have come to learn that's how Jesus works with me personally; He doesn't rush me and oftentimes lets me jump right in only to have to throw me a life line again. There is hope in Christ no matter how "new" you may feel you are, so keep reading, He is training you for a specific purpose.

Whispers from the Devil

"The thief comes only to steal, kill and destroy"

—John 10:10a (KJV)

IT WAS IN this phase of my life that I began to drink from the well of rebellion. Ah, what a sweet tasting liquid, but the change that is brought upon the face of the consumer is that of arrogance and anger. For a plethora of reasons, I began to pursue many sexual escapades with different women and at the end of that road. I found myself sitting in an abortion clinic, holding the hand of my then eighteen-year-old girlfriend as the doctor took away the life we had brought into this world. I'll never forget walking out of that old house in downtown Memphis where they murder babies, and I had played a part in the destruction of my own child. God have mercy on me. After she took a few steps, she fell to her knees and began vomiting. I picked her up in both arms and carried her like a baby to the car. I'll never forget looking across the street at the picketers as they lowered their "*No abortion*" signs and wept for me and my girlfriend.

Even as I write this I remember thinking, "How did I get here?" The truth is that I was not willing to face the music concerning what I did. Nobody put a gun to my head and said, "have sex with her," that was my decision and now we were faced with the consequences and the low and dark places of seeing the destruction of sin. God is able to bring about beauty from ashes—my step-son, Christopher, is about the exact age my child would have been if we had not ended the pregnancy. There is always some form of hope, if you're looking.

It was not too long after that horrific time that she and I split up, and I began pursuing music as a way to forget and numb the pain. I had always loved singing, and now I had been playing rock music with some friends for a while. One day a buddy of mine whom I had been doing music with asked if I'd help him move. With nothing else to do, I said, "Sure." Well, after the work was done, he pulled out a bottle of what appeared to be pink pills. It turned out they were 10 mg Lortabs. He gave me one, and without hesitating, I took it and that began my journey into the wilderness of drugs.

Pills made me feel like I was Superman. Never mind the withdrawal pain that I would feel the next day and the "no-holds-barred," "anything goes" pursuit I would make to get more; in the beginning, it was seemingly innocent fun. I really began to dig deep into the whole rock band thing at this time of my life, and the pills and alcohol would take me to a pseudo-level of energy and euphoria on stage, but I began to notice would die down a little each time, and I found myself chasing that original high with no success. Life was like a roller coaster, but nobody was allowed off, sure it was fun the first few go rounds but now you want to get off. I found myself at parties where cocaine, pills, and alcohol were as common as Gatorade at a track meet. I realized soon enough I was spinning out of control and being a lead singer of a band didn't help in the area of humbling down and asking for help.

"Functional addict" is a title that could have been applied to my life at this time. In my early twenties, I was still working for a sales company making way more money than a kid with a drug problem should make. I would finish my weeks' work, which was fueled—energetically speaking—by pills of course, then it was off to the New Daisy, The Hard Rock Café, or some spot to do music and dope every weekend. Don't get me wrong, I'm not saying that being in a band means you'll become a junkie—not the case at all—but in my case, it fueled that lifestyle I had already began years ago. Suddenly I could barely make out the day from the night, nor could I make out the places I would wake up in or the people I'd wake up next to. The devil had definitely tightened the last notch on the leash he had around my neck. Ah, but thank God for parents and others who were praying for me at this wild and yet fragile time of my life. Nearing the end of my twenty-third year of life on this planet, I had quit my good sales job, took out my entire 401k, and was about to dive into Satan's swimming pool of drugs, death, and destruction. The Bible says, "The thief cometh not but to steal, kill and destroy." Jesus also says in that same verse, "I have come that ye might have life, and life abundantly." There's no doubt that the enemy of our souls had me in his crosshairs and still does today but there's victory in Jesus. I know because, here I am. This again brings me to the subject of the necessity of prayer for our children. Our prayers and life-example may be the only thing between them and the devil. If it were not for the prayers and examples of my family, I too would be a lost soul. Please pray for our children they are bombarded on a daily basis with pornographic and social temptation and our prayers may be the only thing between them and ultimate destruction. Let's live this abundant life in front of our children, finding joy in Jesus and showing them there is a better way.

Numbing God's Knock on My Heart

"Behold, I stand at the door, and knock: if any man
hear my voice, and open the door, I will come in to
him, and sup with him, and he with me."

—Revelation 3:20 (KJV)

IT WAS ABOUT two in the afternoon when a former work
buddy and I had just bought some heroin with money we
got from the pawn shop selling items we'd stolen earlier
that day. He was an experienced junkie; I had never done
heroin before, but the string of bad decisions and the trail
of wounded people I had left behind was enough for me
to welcome something that seemed to promise to make

all the pain go away, but something I said I'd never do: the needle. He told me to make a fist as he tied a rubber tourniquet around my arm. He said, "Look away." I felt the needle prick into my arm and suddenly the dashboard I was staring at seemed to move far, far away. Before I even knew what was happening, we were already driving down the street. I remember buildings looking like shadows and the sound of the wind was like a demon trying to sing a worship song. It was all wrong, but it was too late—I was already in the beast.

The next year or so was almost a complete blur; the only memories I have are the rushes of adrenaline from numerous scares either by almost getting caught stealing, or almost dying from overdoses. Many times my parents would let me back into their home, hoping to help me, only to be heartbroken again when they would wake up to find me gone and money absent from their wallets and purses. One day stands out strong in my mind: I was sitting in a dope house (an abandoned and condemned building). I had run out of heroin, and my body began to experience withdrawal. If it had not been for a fellow druggie there with a car, I probably would have died. Hours after cold sweats and my bowels releasing uncontrollably on myself, he pulled up to the Med downtown and rolled me out of his car, face down onto the emergency driveway, then took off. It was like I was in some horrible movie. I remember blood coming out of my nose and mouth, slowly trickling away from my face, and I was too tired to get up. The last thing I remember is hearing someone scream, "*We got one, he's on the driveway!*" I woke up to a masked man holding what seemed to be two pads with cords coming out, and the masked man said, "*He's back!*" I was defibrillated back to life. Thank you, God, for second, third, and fourth chances! Why me though? A worthless thieving junkie; but God saw the end from the beginning.

You would think that would have woke up, but I left the hospital and immediately ran back into the arms of that cold-souled woman known as heroin. I've come to learn that God is relentless in His pursuit of us; if it's not your time to die, He's not going to let you, no matter how badly you want to. Unfortunately, I have plenty of personal stories to prove that theory. After my hospital incident, I went back to that same dope house, and with my last fifty dollars, I bought a pack of heroin and some cocaine. I remember feeling what most addicts feel at this point: a desperation to die; you're not getting high anymore; you're just running from the withdrawals. I remember it like it was yesterday. Night had come and I was sitting at a table, and the only light was from a candle in front of me. I mixed up the coke and water into my needle and shot it into my vein. I honestly thought there was an earthquake in Memphis because the walls and the table that I was looking at started to shake violently. What snapped me back to reality was when I put my hand on my chest and I felt my heart pounding into my hand. I realized that I was seizing from too much pure cocaine. The next thing I remember I was being grabbed out of the chair by the guy who was running drugs out of the house. He was making his best effort to get me out because, you see, if I died, at least I wouldn't be in the house he was selling out of. At this point, I remember crying out to God for help. Once I got outside, I actually started to calm down and the seizure stopped. Revelation 3:20 Jesus says, "behold, I stand at the door and knock." I believe that every time I stuck that needle into my arm, I was quieting that knock. After several near-death overdoses, I found myself in a hotel room, and heroin had become hard to find, so I got some OxyContin and some "glass", otherwise known as crystal meth. I'll spare you the gory details, but to make a long story short I stayed awake for two weeks in that room, and the things I saw—demonically speaking—were enough to let me know the devil is real, and he ultimately wanted me dead. I passed out for what had to have been two days and woke up again in a puddle of my own waste. I remember taking a shower, leaving the room with a bottle of water and a granola bar, and headed out on foot, not knowing where I was going—but God did. Not too long afterward, I found myself on Crump Boulevard looking for a homeless shelter I had heard about. Little did I know my life was about to change dramatically, and the change would be brought about by God himself.

Gone but Not Forgotten

"For He hath said, 'I will never leave thee,
nor forsake thee.'"

—Hebrews 13:5b (KJV)

THE BIBLE SAYS in Proverbs 21:1 "The king's heart is in the Hand of the Lord, He turns it where He wishes, like the rivers of water He turns it". Little did I know that on September 18, 2005, God was about to turn my heart away from drugs and toward him. I was walking down Crump Blvd and as the saying goes I was "tore up from the floor up," and before I had reached an old bridge, a taxi cab pulled up next to me and I got in. The driver turned around and looked at me with pity in his eyes as if I were the most pathetic thing he'd ever seen, but of course, I didn't realize how bad off I had gotten. Without asking me where I wanted to go, he shook his head and said, "*Lord have mercy, I know some people who can help you.*" He drove me up to 3rd Street, took a left, and pulled up to a shelter for the homeless. The driver said, "*Son, go knock on that door. They'll help you.*" It still hadn't dawned on me what was happening. I mean, how often does a taxi give you a free ride anywhere? So I got out and walked up to the door and knocked. Even though about fifteen seconds had passed no one came to the door, I decided to turn around and thank the taxi driver, and as I turned around, the taxi had vanished—it was gone! I didn't even hear him leave! Right about the time I walked to the sidewalk to look down both ends of the street to see where this "ghost taxi" had gone, I heard someone behind me say, "*Hey! Was you knockin' on this door?*" I turned around again to see a six-foot-three black man standing in the doorway. He looked at me like the taxi driver did and said, "*Lord have mercy. Come on in, boy.*" The Lord was turning my heart right there on that 3rd Street sidewalk, and as I walked through the door of that shelter, I didn't know it then, but God was about to perform open heart surgery on my soul.

While following this tall man through the door of this homeless shelter (or as I'd like to call it "Hospital for the Sick Soul"), I heard a loud voice screaming out, "*God loved you. He still loves you. He ain't gave up on you, don't give up on yourself!*" As I entered this big room full of sherbert orange church pews, reality started sinking in. Here I was, a twenty-five-year-old, 115-pound junkie kid sitting down with a bunch of old homeless men who looked as if they were dead bodies breathing. I sat down, and the tall man told me stay and listen to the preacher. "*I'll get you something to eat in a minute,*" he said. As I sat there I could have sworn the preacher, who wearing a white shirt and white pants was talking directly to me. He was screaming to me of God's great love, demonstrated in his Son's death, and I remember feeling like someone threw water on my face. I wiped my face with my hands to realize I was crying and didn't even know it. It was as if my soul was crying. My body was certainly too tired and weak to muster up any emotion or tears, and it was as if my soul said, "I give up!" After wiping my face, I remember looking at my hands, clothes, and feet; and everything started to make sense and I understood why the taxi driver and the other people at this shelter were looking at me the way they were—I was covered in dirt! The lines in the palm of my hands were filthy. I had sandals on, and my feet were covered with dirt. I'll never forget that preacher in his white clothes reaching down mid-sermon, picking me up out of the seat and praying for me. I cried, just as I am crying now, as I write this. Jesus began to remove the scales that had blinded my eyes, and He was filling my cold, sinful heart up with his warm liquid love.

During the next few weeks, I would miraculously dodge the withdrawal bullet and was very thankful to God for that because nothing pulls an addict back in like the need to rid themselves of the horrific nightmare of withdrawals. I believe Jesus did me that favor, as if to say, "I'll spare you the withdrawals if you'll follow me." I'm glad I did. I don't know why I was spared that painful process; I wish everyone who wanted to get clean was, but maybe it was just time. The joy of seeing my family on scheduled visit days by the shelter was wonderful. They all came out, and we'd sit and talk and laugh, something I had forgotten how to do. The Bible also says, "Laughter is like good medicine," and God knew I needed a lot of it. I praise the Lord for the incredible restoration of my family at that time, and for their amazing ability to forgive me. All through October, I worked for the shelter and received twenty dollars a week, then on Sunday I'd go to church, and services lasted about five hours, but you need it like that when you're in recovery. I had opportunity to play drums, and in his own mysterious way, God was leading me back to my love for music. October 27, 2005, rolled around, I had my first court date and I went to Goodwill with my family the day before to get a suit for court. I was feeling wonderful and put back together again, as a man—finally! However, little did I know on that morning, when I stepped out of that homeless shelter van that had given me a ride to 201 Poplar for court and as I walked up the steps to the courthouse, little did I know it would be the last time I would be a resident of that shelter. God had used his mighty warriors at that shelter to do a work in my life that prepared me for the dungeon which was awaiting me.

For anyone reading this who has a loved one in addiction and doesn't understand the concept of withdrawals, let me help you out a little bit. It's as if fire ants are crawling through your veins while your body goes from extremely hot and sweaty to freezing cold—as if someone is throwing ice and fire on you every few minutes. If that wasn't enough, if enough strength could be found to sit on the toilet, your body will go through horrific diarrhea—and get a trash can ready because vomiting occurs at the same time. To add insult to injury, depression becomes your state of mind. So it's an attack on your soul, spirit, and body.

The Dungeon

"I cried unto God with my voice, even unto God
with my voice; and he gave ear unto me"

—Psalm 77:1 (KJV)

I WALKED INTO the tall building known as 201 Poplar to
face a misdemeanor that I had gotten months prior because
of my drug lifestyle. I entered the courtroom to schedule
payment for my fines. I was not expecting any prison time,
but as I was leaving, two detectives busted into the courtroom, holding a picture and looking for a guy with a tattoo
on his neck. It was almost like the slow motion part of mov-
ies where a war is about to start and everything slows down.
I remember one of the officers grabbing my arm, twisting
me around, and slamming me into a wall; the other one

saying "*We got him*" into a walkie-talkie and then screaming at me "*don't move!*" Even as I was pinned against the wall and yelled at while being handcuffed, I felt a strange peace wash all over me from my head to my feet, and I knew then that even though I was reaping what I had sown, the Lord was with me and was going to use this to make me a better man. After taking a few breaths and as they tightening the cuffs on my wrist, I said, "*Guys, you don't have to do this. I'm ready.*" I'll never forget the look on that detective's face; it was as if he knew I had been free from the rebellious criminal spirit that he thought he was going to arrest.

After about an hour of being shuffled from one room to the other, I wound up in an office with these two detectives. Another detective had join their group, and he was pounding the table, yelling at me, saying things like "*We have all the evidence here. You better be honest or you're going to be put away for a long time!*" Again, the strange peace of God was on me, and I said, "*Sir, if you give me a pencil, a piece of paper, a Coca-Cola, and a Snickers bar, I'll tell you everything that I can remember stealing.*" I knew that once I confessed to my crimes, I would probably not taste a Coca-Cola or a Snickers bar for many years to come. To make a long story short, after admitting to the catalog of crimes that I had committed in the summer of 2005, I was then escorted to the jail where I was processed, given a number and a bag of state-issued prison clothes, and a few toiletry items. The process of going from citizen to prisoner is comparable to a cow headed to the slaughter. You're tagged, given a number, and told to get in line. Don't get me wrong, I needed to go there, I needed to go even further into losing the identity of whoever I thought I was so that more of Danny could be emptied out, and more of God could be poured in.

I spent about six months in that county jail, battling court case after court case to finally receive a sentence of ten years in Tennessee, of which I only served two before being paroled out. However, it was in those two years of prison, God taught me valuable lessons that are still with me today—one of which is thankfulness. It's nice to choose what you want to eat, to sleep on a bed that is not one inch thick, to shut the door and have some privacy when you go to the bathroom, to not be yelled at to hurry up because you only have two minutes left for eating.

Finally, God also taught me one more valuable lesson before I left Memphis to go to yet another portion of a dungeon, in another state. God began teaching me the value in and the great need we have in his Son, Jesus. Amidst the letters I wrote home for guys who couldn't write, the letters I read to guys who couldn't read from their family, the Bible studies I was blessed to lead, and the visits with my own family through plated glass, God formed in me through all of those trials and tribulations not only the manifestation of Christ in me, but a great love for his Word. After being in Memphis prison for two years, I thought I was going to head home for a couple days and enjoy some down time with my family before turning myself into Mississippi for charges I had there. But the day I was released from Memphis, a Mississippi squad car was waiting for me. The officer chained my ankles and my hands to my waist and then put chains over my shoulders connecting to my waist. Even while covered in chains, the wind was knocked out of me from realizing I wasn't going home for couple days; that strange sense of peace fell upon me again in the back of that squad car. I didn't know it then, but God was escorting me to a place where he would bring me to an even higher level of intimate relationship with himself. God began to turn these dungeons into palaces, and it was because he was there with me.

I remember riding in that squad car from Shelby County in Tennessee to DeSoto County in Mississippi, and even though I was battling anger—because I thought I was going home, and it turned out that I wasn't—I couldn't help but remember how awesome the Lord had been to me in prison in Memphis. If you're reading this book and you think that you are in too dark of a situation for God to move or to use you, then think again. Before I get into telling you how awesomely God moved in the bowels of Mississippi allow me, if you would for a moment, to reminisce on the favor he poured out on this prisoner's life in a Memphis prison. While I was in the county jail in Memphis, I began to write lyrics to a lot of songs and only had the music in my head. During Bible studies and things we called prayer circles where as many guys who wanted to would gather in a circle to pray, I would take the opportunity to try out some of my songs. I would usually find a table to do a drum beat on, and over the course of the four years I spent in prison, I had formed a pretty formidable callus on my left wrist where I would beat on the table to create a drum beat and then I would sing the song. Oftentimes, I would notice when a sermon or a prayer request or something like that wouldn't pierce through and get people's attention, usually a good song would. I remember one incident in particular when a guard asked me at Christmas time to go and sing to different pods, which are rooms full of prisoners, and even though I was burdened with sadness myself missing my family at Christmas time, sitting in prison, I went ahead and did it; and I don't know how, but God somehow gave me a peace that I couldn't understand. While singing into the actual rooms with sixty sometimes seventy prisoners, you can imagine me being a prisoner. Some of them could care less to hear it, but there were a few here and there whom you could tell it was ministering to, and if one person could be touched, it was worth it for me. I still try to live that way outside of prison, sometimes in ministering or singing, you look around and see some people's faces that appear, which appear as though they could care less about what you are saying, but there are always those few—sometimes a lot of—people whom you can tell really need it and are hungry for a message of hope.

Once I had finally made it to the actual DeSoto County, MS prison to start serving my time, (I was also given ten years in Mississippi) it wasn't even a month later that I wound up in a drug program building doing the same thing I did at the county jail, beating on tables and singing praises to God. A counselor named Mr. Petty took notice after I had joined up with about five other guys, and we started writing songs and working out harmonies. The next thing you know, he got a guitar donated to the drug program, and we started writing songs with real music, and I actually got to hear what was in my head come to fruition. The Lord opened doors for us to go all around to different parts of the prison and even sing and minister to guards and staff members! We were once invited out to a Christmas dinner for the prison staff, and we sang for about an hour and thirty minutes, then afterward we were allowed to get a tray of Piccadilly's cafeteria–catered food, and to a group of prisoners who had been eating prison food for years, this was like heaven on earth. One of the memories that stands out in my mind the most is a day when we were asked by one of the guards to bring the guitar and sing some songs for a man who had been put in solitary confinement, and when we approached the metal door the inmate was behind, we could hear him screaming obscenities, hitting the wall and yelling, and as soon as I hit the strings on the guitar and we began singing, it got strangely quiet. We got toward the end of the song and the lyrics to it at the end we're "*Lord you picked me up you turned me around you made me whole.*" I remember I was playing the music to it, and we kept singing that line over and over again, and the harmonies echoing against the walls were beautiful, and it felt like the angels of the Lord were with us in that hallway. The most amazing part of that story is that a few days later, that man who had pretty much seemed to have lost his mind was released into general population where he could be around other prisoners and not be a harm to them or himself, and I saw him in church service later that day, sitting down, calm, and in what appeared to be his right mind. That was one of the times that God helped me see that even though my crimes had gotten me there, he was still going to use me there for his glory.

While at Mississippi, the Lord really opened my eyes to something inside myself that I had not noticed; there was a part of me that thought because I was worshipping God so much, he would give me some extra favor and let me get out early. I look back now and laugh, but then it was no laughing matter. I wanted to go home badly, but God knew there was more he needed to do in my heart. Once I had reached the county jail in Mississippi and had gotten booked into their system, they sent me to H pod, which was supposed to have about fifty inmates, but because of overcrowding, there were about a 125 to that pod. I remember dragging the bed they gave me into cell number 14, a cell big enough barely for two people, but I found that I would be the third man in that cell sleeping on the floor for the next two weeks. Eventually one of the guys was released to go serve his time somewhere else, and I got off the floor. You would have thought it was a Christmas present! Once I had finally gotten over my anger that I wasn't going home, I began to seek God again, but this time to find out who he was—whether I went home or not. I will tell you this much, I saw things happen in that prison through worship that I have yet to see happen out here in the free world where people can go home when they want to, eat what they want, and do what they want when they want. He showed me that it's in the dark trials of life when we choose to worship God instead of complaining, that's when he steps in and the miraculous happens. I had gang members come to my cell and give me free coffee and honey buns, asking me to sit and drink coffee with them, and tell them more about Jesus. It was almost unbelievable! I saw people let go of their gang affiliations and grab hold of Jesus, grown men with tears falling down their face as the Lord touched their hearts with grace for the first time!

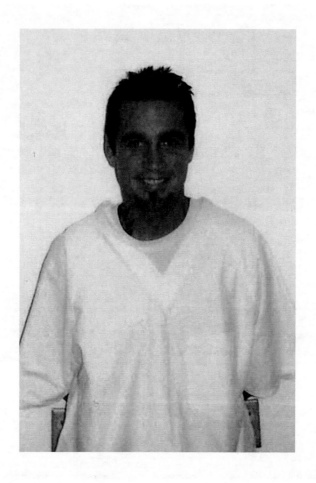

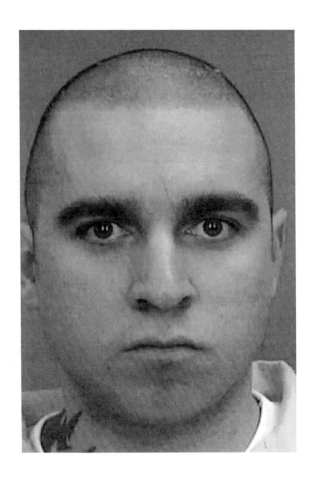

"EVERY PART OF SCRIPTURE IS GOD-BREATHED & USEFUL ONE WAY OR ANOTHER— SHOWING US TRUTH, EXPOSING OUR REBELLION, CORRECTING OUR MISTAKES, TRAINING US TO LIVE GOD'S WAY.

THROUGH THE WORD WE ARE PUT TOGETHER & SHAPED UP FOR THE TASKS GOD HAS FOR US."

2 TIMOTHY 3:16-17
(THE MESSAGE)

inSTATUSap

Love ya's for always... momma

Dont try to out argue the devil
when the devil tells us we'ee not
worthy - just tell him to take
the argument up with the blood
of Jesus
& walk
away

MISSISSIPPI PAROLE BOARD

Jackson, Mississippi

CERTIFICATE OF PAROLE

KNOW ALL MEN BY THESE PRESENTS:

It having been made to appear to the State Parole Board that ___COSBY, DANNY LEE JR___

_____, Register No. __133633__ _____, a prisoner in the Mississippi

DEPARTMENT OF CORRECTIONS is eligible to be PAROLED and that there is a
reasonable probability that said prisoner WILL REMAIN AT LIBERTY WITHOUT VIOLATING
THE LAWS, and it being the opinion of the State Parole Board that the release of this prisoner
is not incompatible with the welfare of society it is ORDERED by the said State Parole Board
that the prisoner be PAROLED from the MISSISSIPPI DEPARTMENT OF CORRECTIONS
ON _____**NOVEMBER 24**_____ , 20 __09__ _____ and that said
prisoner is paroled to __**TIPTON, TN**__ _____ to remain there until
properly transferred by Mississippi Department of Corrections personnel or until expiration or
revocation of said parole, or in event of arrest and conviction for law violation, until action has
been taken by the State Parole Board.

Witness our signature and seal, this _____8ᵗʰ_____ day
SEPTEMBER   **2009**

MDOC Commissary - Order Form

Inmate Number

Facility: _____

Building: _____ Zone: _____ Bed: _____

Name: _____

Signature: _____

Officer Signature: _____

Marking Instructions

- Use a No. 2 pencil or blue or black ink pen only.
- Do not use pens with ink that soaks through the paper.
- Make solid marks that fill the oval completely.   CORRECT MARK ●
- Make no stray marks on this form.
- Do not fold, tear, or mutilate this form.   INCORRECT MARKS ⊘ ⊗ ◓ ◔

Item 1		Item 2		Item 3		Item 4		Item 5	
Inventory ID	QTY	Inventory ID	QTY	Inventory ID	QTY	Inventory ID	QTY	Inventory ID	QTY

Item 6		Item 7		Item 8		Item 9		Item 10	
Inventory ID	QTY	Inventory ID	QTY	Inventory ID	QTY	Inventory ID	QTY	Inventory ID	QTY

Item 11		Item 12		Item 13		Item 14		Item 15	
Inventory ID	QTY	Inventory ID	QTY	Inventory ID	QTY	Inventory ID	QTY	Inventory ID	QTY

WEdNEsdAy, AuqusT 16, 1995

Perfect Love

God demonstrated perfect love at the Cross. While all people stand guilty of sin, God stands ready to pardon all sin. Nothing but the blood of Jesus received as Gods judgement for sin will suffice. God gave his precious sinless Son for yours and my sins. It is truly, "Amazing Grace" that is still reaching to anyone. Who will come Gods way.

Jesus, Gods perfect love.
Church of God of Prophecy
Pastor Danny Cosby, SC
1270 Stage Rd.
Bible search 10:30 AM - 11:15 AM
Worship 11:15 AM - 12:15 PM

Momma,
I'm Comin' Home

"Therefore if any man be in Christ,
he is a new creature: old things are passed away;
behold, all things are become new." (KJV)

IN MISSISSIPPI THERE seemed to be a cloud of depression and anxiety floating above everywhere I was, so it seemed to be that much more difficult to really enjoy praise and worship. However, it was in those cold, gray dungeons of Mississippi that God taught me the priceless skill of praising him, even when I didn't feel like it. The most difficult time was probably served in Greenwood, Mississippi, the trip to that prison involved a lot of stops, searches, and something called processing where you are thrown in a line of other inmates, you all get your heads shaved, shower together, and have clothes and bags of peanut butter sandwiches thrown at you like you're an animal. Once you've made it through the line of processing, they snap your picture and once you've gone through that hell, you're not a happy camper, so everybody who sees the mug shot says, "Wow! You look like a real criminal. You looked angry, not having any idea what in the world you went through." Once I made it to Greenwood, I was marched off the prison bus, unchained, and given a tray of what they said was food. It was some kind of brown liquid with what appeared to be possibly meat floating in it, a yellow substance that I think was pudding, and two pieces of bread. Greenwood, Mississippi, was definitely not famous for good food. After about an hour of sitting in a room with four other inmates, I was given a bag of pants with black and white stripes on them, some towels, a bar soap, and a toothbrush. I was then marched to a building, and once inside you would have thought it was the Coliseum back in Roman days with all of the noise of people screaming and talking to each other, echoing off the concrete walls and floors. I was first put in pod A for about two weeks, which I later found out was called the throwaway pod because there were no drug programs or anything going on in that pod, just a bunch of men eating, sleeping, and doing time. It's a huge misconception that there is a lot of opportunity for rehabilitation in prison because there isn't. You basically have to want to do better yourself and then take the appropriate measures like getting books and finding out for yourself if there are any classes anywhere to take. Well, about the third week of my stay in Greenwood, Mississippi, at the prison called Delta Correctional Facility, otherwise known as DCF, I remember going to lunch, which basically is you being herded in like a cow to the slaughter. I remember sitting at a metal table with three other inmates, and the table was probably large enough for only two to sit at comfortably. After you sit down, you're given about three minutes to eat your meal while a seemingly disgruntled and angry guard yells at the entire row to hurry up and finish! Don't get me wrong, if I was a guard in a prison with men who mostly don't care about trying to do right, I would probably be angry and impatient as well; however, for the very few of us who were trying to be respectful and had realized we had done wrong and we're trying to change, it was quite a hellish experience on a daily basis. Well, one day in particular I was walking back to the pod and in Greenwood, Mississippi, when you are not in a gang, you have to be in the middle of the line because certain gang members own the front of the line and the other gang members own the end of the line, and if you are anywhere in the front or back and are not in their gang, they tax you by taking your commissary items or just simply beating you up. Well, I was in the middle of the line, walking back and the chaplain of the prison was trying to exit the door we were walking through. I stopped to let him through, knowing that I would probably pay a price for it. I could hear talking coming from the back of the line, and I knew that I was getting myself into hot water, but I felt like the Lord was doing something at that moment. The chaplain said thank you, walked through the door, and after I started marching again, he said, "Hey, you come here." He asked me a few questions about myself and then said how would you like to be in my faith-based pod? I said sure, but you're going to have to walk me back to the pod because if I get in the back of that line, they're going to pretty much beat me up. So he did, and that very day I was moved to the faith-based pod.

I stayed in that pod for nearly over a year and took courses that taught me how to memorize chapters of the Bible, and even got the opportunity to play music with real instruments for church services. However, in Greenwood, Mississippi, most inmates would go to church just to get out of the pod and could really care less about what you were trying to sing or play at church, and you could tell by the looks on their faces. However, it was through these so-called worship services that God taught me to lead people into worship, people who really could care less about whether I lived or not, and let me tell you something—you learn a lot, and stuff starts to change and happen inside of you when you're leading worship in front of a bunch of people who look like they would rather you be dead. I took a course called Institute of Self-worth while I was in this prison, which basically radically changed my viewpoint on God's grace, and I was released in my spirit from having to do better to make God love me more, and I realized for the first time in my life that God loved me, whether I got it right or not and knowing that helped me to get it right more often. Chaplin Speight was a man of few words, but I think besides Jesus Christ himself, this man made the strongest impact on my life than anybody I have ever met. He wasn't about patting you on the back and telling you how good you did; he just expected you to do what you were supposed to do. However, on very rare occasions, you would see him cry as he talked about the love of Jesus, and every once in awhile you might get a pat on the back, and that would keep you good for another three months or so. I'll never forget the day I left DCF. They announced over the speakers for me to get my things together and after the chaplin got to the pod for the day's regular lessons, he got the entire pod, which then circled me for about sixty minutes and prayed over me. I felt like somebody was pouring hot oil into my heart. It was a feeling I'll never forget. After that, somebody asked me to sing one last song, and out of every song running through my head I decided to sing a stanza of the chaplain page's favorite song, "Spirit of the Living God Fall Afresh on Me." After I open my eyes singing it, I saw chap with tears running down his face. This man, in my humble opinion, had to be the closest to the character of Christ that I had ever been around in my life, and I was actually sad to leave being around him. After getting changed up again and rushed onto a bus like a cow going to the slaughter, not knowing where I was going about an hour later, the bus pulled up to a prison called Parchman, which is pretty famous in Mississippi for being hell on earth. I stayed here a week before I found out from a counselor that I was transferring to something called a satellite, which is a minimum security prison, and you exchange your black- and white-striped pants for green- and white-striped pants. I spent the next several months here cooking for eighty prisoners, making new friendships and leading worship in a much more relaxed environment. Everything was better here. The food, the ability to go outside when you wanted to, and they even left the gate open, and right down the driveway was a residential neighborhood! You may wonder why would they do that, but once you make it to this prison, you know that you're on your way home soon. I saw a lot of guys go home on parole out of the kitchen window. I can see the parking lot where they would leave with their families, get in the car, and leave. I had built a good relationship with the parole counselor just simply talking with her about the Word of God, and I realized that even though some people were free from prison, they were in a prison in their mind.

Well, it was around the middle of October, and the parole counselor called me into her office and said, "Danny, I have a surprise for you. Can you guess what it is?" I said,

"My parole papers?" Jokingly, of course. Because by this time, I had only served a little over two years in Mississippi and was sure that I would do at least another year or so on a ten-year sentence. Well, she pulled an envelope out of her desk and said, "Congratulations! You've been approved for parole!" Goosebumps shot down the back of my neck, and I jumped out of my skin! I got to call home and tell Mom, and she was of course excited. Looking back now, I'm sure she was probably a little nervous, wondering what was going to happen. The next several weeks until November the 24th, which was the day they let me go, I spent my days reading scripture, praising God, cooking and training up another cook, and I'll be honest—it seemed like the time dragged by slowly when I knew I was getting out.

I always tried to give it my best when cooking for the prisoners. I would use garlic powder, salt, pepper, and other seasonings when they were available to make the meal as tasty as possible, because I remembered how bland everything was that I ate everywhere else I did time. I remember the last meal I cooked for them. I made a hamburger meal with macaroni and cheese and vanilla cake with vanilla icing, and icing was a rarity because most cooks could care less to dress up a cake with icing. I took a dollar of my money that I had because in this prison, you were allowed a few bucks for vending machines. I bought two Butterfinger candy bars, crushed them up, and sprinkled them over the vanilla icing on the cake. Well, when the guys were ready to eat dinner, you would have thought it was the Fourth of July. They were freaking out about the Butterfinger vanilla cake, and some of them said, "Danny, I'm glad you made parole, but please show this other guy how you do what you do because the meals he has cooked when you're not cooking are terrible!" Anyway, the last day that I was there, I remember a friend of mine named Chris Stewart who was blessed to have a job cleaning up and maintaining a local college, in minimum security prisons; oftentimes, inmates have jobs outside of the prison during the day. Well, I didn't know it, but he had made arrangements for me to join him that day. The paperwork was signed, and I went to the college with him to hang out. The dean of the college had gotten very close to Chris, and he made a steak lunch with baked potato and Dr Pepper for us—and let me tell you something, after years of eating prison food, that steak was like God's own butter in my mouth. It was a great way to spend the last day because Chris and I had become very close friends during this time. The next day, I woke up, ate some eggs and biscuits, and got my things together, waiting for my mother to come pick me up. She arrived about 8:15 on November 24, 2009. She brought a change of clothes for me. I got into them, and as I said good-bye to the few prisoners and one guard who were there, I took my first step out the door toward freedom. It's true. The air smells different when you've been set free! I remember walking down the driveway and through the open gates with the little barbed wire on top of them that I wasn't allowed to go past before, but nobody stopped me this time. It was over; I had served my time. As I got into my mother's Toyota Tercel and looked at her with a wide-eyed eyes and a big grin, I couldn't help but wonder with joy and some fear what would be next.

A New Beginning

"Behold, I will do a new thing; now it shall spring
forth; shall ye not know it? I will even make a way
in the wilderness, and rivers in the desert."

—Isaiah 43:19 (KJV)

THEY SAY ABOUT 90 percent of the men and women
released from prison go back after three to six months of
their release. I thank God that as I'm writing this book to
you, I am now coming up on almost four years of being
out of that dungeon. It definitely helps to have a good support system when you get out, which is why I think most
go back because they get out, and they have no one there
with open arms waiting for them to support and believe
in their recovery. Pray if you would please for programs to

pop up that help men and women getting out of prison to return to society and become productive law-abiding citizens again. Also pray that the men and women that get out are focused and have a desire to stay out and to not involve themselves in a life of crime ever again. As we drove away from the prison in Corinth, Mississippi, I remember feeling the pull to look back and look at it one last time, but I didn't, and I don't know if it was the thought of how Lot's wife turned around to look at the burning city of Sodom and Gomorrah, and turned into a pillar of salt, or if it was God saying what is behind you is behind you, everything now is in front of you. Either way, I will never forget the excited yet fearful feeling that I had as we were driving down that road back to Memphis.

Our first stop was at my sister's house in Oakland, Tennessee, my brother-in-law met us at the door with a hug and we walked in, and he gave me a bag of clothes and some cologne. Afterward we traveled to my Aunt Linda's house, where I met her and my Mee-maw. I was greeted with a tray full of sandwiches, a bowl full of potato chips, and some Dr. Pepper! After eating prison food for over four years, this was a fantastic treat. We sat and talked and ate and laughed; it was a real blessing. The next stop would be home, my mom and dad's place in Drummonds, Tennessee. I remember walking in and was greeted by our lab named Man. I remember him pouncing on me and licking me at least thirty-five hundred times! My mom showed me to the room that she had prepared for me; it was beautiful—it was my own room! Decked walls with Bible verse pictures and a king size comfortable bed. No more prison bunk beds, and no more rooms filled with inmates screaming and yelling at each other. Peace finally! After sitting down on the bed and just looking around in amazement, I remember going to the bathroom. I will spare you the details there, but I must tell you that it was truly a blessing to shut the door and to have complete privacy in the restroom by myself. See, in prison, the restrooms, the showers, and toilets have no division walls and no doors; everything is open to everybody in the pod, even the guards. Next, I remember going into the kitchen and loving the fact that I could open the refrigerator door and pick what I wanted to drink or eat. It was the little things when I got out that were amazing to me, just the ability to walk outside whenever I wanted to and go take a walk in the woods and talk to God.

Later that evening, family and friends drove out to my mom and dad's to greet me and to have a welcome back home dinner. It was such a blessing to see everybody, and I remember reading a note that I had written to them while I was in prison to thank them for their support while I was in prison. I barely got halfway through it before I started to cry, and at one point, I had really gotten overwhelmed with so many people being in one place that I had to go take a walk outside and get some air. My sister followed me out and gave me a hug and told me that she was so glad that I was back home. I really wish that everyone who gets out of prison could have a support system like I did; I was truly blessed and still am.

The next day, my mom took me out to get my driver's license renewed and to apply for my social security card. After all of that, we went and ate at a restaurant, and it was really nice just to sit and be served and to have a regular conversation with my mother. The next day, which would make my third day out of prison, my dad took me into Millington to look for work. He dropped me off at Walmart, and I began to work my way down the street, putting in applications. He met me across the street after I had applied at a few places, and just as I was about to give up because of the old cliché that a felon basically won't be able to find work for at least six months out of prison, I hesitantly walked into a restaurant called Wing Hut n' Sum. When I entered the restaurant, there were two girls filling up plastic containers with ranch and bleu cheese, asking me what I wanted. I asked if the manager was anywhere nearby, and they screamed, "Steve, somebody here to see you!" From the back of the restaurant, a guy in an apron walked up and said, "Yeah, what can I do for you?" I reached out my hand to shake his hand and said, "My name is Danny. I've only been out of prison for three days, and I really need a job." You should have seen the look on his face. You would have thought he thought I was going to rob him right there! Looking back now, I guess I could have introduced myself a little more gracefully, but all I knew was to be truthful and honest. His immediate response was that he was overstaffed as it is, and doesn't really need anybody. But in a moment's time, almost when I was about to turn around and leave, I watched Proverbs 21 verse 1 come to fruition. The Bible says, "The Kings heart is in the hand of the Lord, He turns it wherever He wants to." As soon as Steve told me no, his head turned to the left as if God was turning his heart right in front of my face, and when his head turned back to face me, he said, "Look, can you come in at five today?" I'm telling you all the Word works, and God loves to bless his children! Well, you would have thought I was floating off of the ground. Here I was, knowing that most felons cannot get a job in at least the first half a year out of prison, and I had gotten one in three days! I went back at five o'clock, and I was the most joyful dishwashing, hot-wings-cutting guy that you probably would have ever seen in your life! I had a lot of opportunity to minister to people whom I worked with, not by preaching to them, but just by living with joy, them asking me why I was so happy, and then telling them about how I got to where I was right then. I did that for about a month, and even though I only made about eighty to a hundred dollars a week, it was paying my parole fines and giving me a little bit of Mountain Dew and potato chip money.

For the following months, God would take me through the challenges of changing my job from hot-wing-cutter to working for a friend of the family in his painting business. I also met a girl from my past to somehow found out I was out of prison and wind up coming to my parents house to see me, and after attempting to get plugged back into being in a relationship, I realized pretty quickly that I was not ready for that yet. The relationship ended almost as fast as it had began. From that point on, I told God that I was through trying to add a relationship to my life and that I want to focus on serving him and just doing the basics. After painting for a while, the spring showers had kind of put a damper on me being able to make any money as a painter, but one morning I got a call from a friend I had met at the gym I had started working out at, and he said a job opening had suddenly come about where he worked. That day, I started working for an auto parts company. My dad had gotten a hold of an old Buick while I was in prison and told me if I could save my money and get the thing running and street legal, I could have it. Eventually I'd saved up enough money to get the lights and the brakes fixed on it. Finally I was able to go drive myself to work and to church. I had been going to Wednesday night services at Bellevue with my dad since I'd gotten out of prison, but a good friend of mine had told me about a church called Hope Church and invited me out, so I decided to start going. I couldn't believe what I was seeing at this church. It was like a concert was going on, but it was just a regular worship. You are allowed to bring coffee into the sanctuary, and it was a huge yet cozy church. In the rush to follow this, I enjoyed going to church, home, and work. They say after getting out of prison, you should keep your circle of travel small, and I did. Eventually the old Buick brake started to give out again, and my dad decided to give me his truck and he took the Buick. I thank God for my parents who have always been very sacrificial in their lives to everyone, especially their children. Thank you, Mom and Dad. By the time June had rolled around and I have been out of prison for about seven months and some days, I heard about Hope Church having a choir that you could try out for, so I went for it and was accepted in. Up to this point, I had attempted to plug into the worship teams of several different churches, but when they found out I was an ex-con out on parole, the door was suddenly shut.

Rebuilding
Broken Bridges

"And they that shall be of thee shall build
the old waste places: thou shalt raise up
the foundations of many generations; and thou
shalt be called, the repairer of the breach,
the restorer of paths to dwell in."

—Isaiah 58:12 (KJV)

I WASN'T EVEN going to write about this topic, but the Lord keeps pressing on my heart to do so. Don't worry, I'm not going to lecture but rather share from the heart concerning this topic and what I've seen and learned about it. While I was in prison and being subjected to the most challenging situations concerning relationships with other people, I learned quite a bit. In prison you cannot get away from anyone, you're there whether you want to be or not; there's not a door you can walk in and out of to leave the situations that you find yourself in. There is no gas station to go to, no movie theater to go to, no park or trail to go walk and get away for some peace and quiet. However, it was in these types of inescapable situations that I learned how to deal with people and allow God to shape and form my character, especially in the area of patience. I heard a wise man say once that God is more interested in your character than he is in what you want. There was a time in prison I remember sitting down and doing a Bible study, and a guy sat down next to me and said, "Brother Cosby, please don't tell anyone, but I cannot read or write, and I was wondering if you would please write a letter for me to my wife?" I said, "Of course!" Well, as he began to speak the words he wanted me to write down, I couldn't help but get a little teary-eyed as he began to tell his wife through me in this letter he was sorry for all that he had done and how he hoped that this letter would break the years of silence that drugs had plagued their life with. Well, it wasn't a couple weeks after that letter was sent out that he got called down for a visitation—and guess who it was. It was his wife! He came back with tears in his eyes, walked over to me, planting his face into my shoulder, crying like a baby saying, "Thank, you Cosby! God is working on our marriage. She came to see me!" There was another time after I had been transferred to Mississippi and was in a two-man cell with another guy who was well into his 60s, and as time passed by, he came to know that I had a love for the Lord and we would have many discussions about Jesus in that little six-by-nine room. He told me once about his now adult daughter whom he had not seen or spoken to in fourteen years because of the lifestyle he had led. I remember clearly one night after watching him through much pain and sorrow with tears, telling me about how much he missed his daughter. I grabbed his hands and said, "Let's pray that God would bring her to you miraculously." Well, most of my life I have not looked for miracles but rather simply wanted to believe God by faith for the simple things in life.

Well, I kid you not, but the following week during visitation day, they called his name out over the intercom for visitation, and it literally took me and three other inmates, and eventually a guard to convince him that it was his name being called out. He had been in jail over three years by this point and had never once had a visitation, and even though it wasn't anything to laugh about, I couldn't help but to giggle as I watched this sixty-plus-year-old man look back and forth at me and the door as he slowly crept toward the hallway to walk to the visitation room. It almost became like a live event on TV. Everybody in the big room was yelling at him, "Go, man, go! You got a visit!" Well, after about forty minutes had passed, and I heard them buzz the door open to the cell I was in and through the door walked my cellmate as he walked to his bed and sat down, his jaw was literally dropped, and he looked like he had seen a ghost. I asked him if he was okay. To be honest, I had literally forgotten that we had prayed a week earlier, and without skipping a beat, he fell to his knees grabbed his face and began to weep hysterically like a newborn baby! Not knowing exactly what had happened, I got down on my knees, grabbed his arms and said, "Are you okay? What happened?" In a moment's time, he began to scream at the top of his lungs, "*My daughter! My daughter!* It was my daughter. She came to see me! She found me, she still loves me!" As soon as I heard those words, I remembered what we had prayed for. I immediately felt the warm presence of Jesus Christ in that cold room. I put my arms around him and held him as he cried, praising God! See, he had told me when I met him that he knew there was a God but that he didn't believe that God cared at all about him because of how old he was and the life he had led up to that point. God showed him that day that he was intimately concerned and involved in his life specifically! Another time comes to mind when I was finishing up the last of four years in prison. I was in a minimum security prison in Corinth, Mississippi, finally after doing the right things and earning trust from the prison association and getting to leave the maximum security prisons. While I was there, I met a man during a Bible study service from some volunteers who had come out from another church. He had been in prison for about five years once I met him, and after the Bible study as it had always been in my nature I go around and tell each person who was there "God bless" and give them a bro hug. I remembered feeling the hesitant pull back from this guy as I reached out to hug him, but he with reluctance gave me a hug back. Well, over the course of a few months, I began to have more studies and conversations with this guy, and one Sunday after family visitation hours were over with, he walked up to me with tears in his eyes and could barely get out a word of what he was trying to tell me. So I sat down at the table we were at and told him to sit down, and once he finally gathered himself together, he said, "Danny, today my wife and two sons came to visit me and during the time I have known you without even recognizing it, I have been hugging my sons when they leave visitation—and that was something I had never done their entire life. I was raised to believe a man isn't supposed to hug another man even if they are related. Today my youngest son handed me a piece of paper with some words he had written on it, and once I read it, I realized that it was a suicide letter. I looked up at him, wondering what this meant, and once I did, he, my oldest son, and my wife were all crying. I asked him what this meant, and he said, "Daddy, I thought you never really loved me because you never hugged me, and I've been depressed because of it lately and wanted to kill myself, but for the last few months, every time we come out, you hug us and I ask Mom and told her about what I wanted to do, and so I decided to tell you today that I don't want to kill myself because I feel like you love me now."

Well, as you might have guessed, I broke down like a little baby too because God showed me in that moment the power of his love and the great need there is for us men to be willing to let God love others through us! Well, as I bring this chapter to a close, I have one more example I would like to share with you. Once I was released from prison, I spent the first six months working, going to church, and trying to get the basics of regular everyday life down after being locked up for over four years. In that time, I had met someone from my past, and she and I began to attempt to work on a relationship with each other. However, we both realized it just wasn't working, and we split up. It was extra tough for her because she expressed interest in marriage, which I wasn't ready for. I struggled, trying to let her see things from my point of view, but she would have none of it. God was teaching me and her something; I learned that no experience you go through is a waste of time, no matter how much it may seem like it is. After that, I had determined that I would never pursue a relationship with someone ever again, and if God wanted me to be with someone, he would have to put neon flashing light arrows over that woman so that it would be completely clear. Well, in June of 2010, I decided to join the choir at Hope Church, and later on you will read the story of how I met the woman I would marry one day, but the reason I bring it up now is for this principle God has taught me concerning relationships. It's when we let go of trying to find someone to be with to cure the loneliness, throw in the towel on our own efforts, and really literally give it over to God that he is finally able to show us whether we need to stay single and enjoy his grace in that area, or he is finally able to bring who he made for us to us. I know this sounds very pie in the sky and cliche if you're going through a lonely time or an ugly divorce or whatever, but it's my job I believe to express to you what I have seen work in my own life. Relationships are so much more than having your loneliness cured; it's about learning how to be okay with it being just you and God and then resolving to let God do whatever he wants or to bring whoever he wants. I believe that is one of the most powerful messages Jesus gives us concerning what he did for us on the cross. He willingly let himself be killed so that we could have a relationship with God again. The Bible says that God demonstrated his love toward us in this way. While we were sinners, Christ died for the ungodly! It was all about relationship! God wanted a relationship with us, but sin entered and destroyed our relationship. I know it's not easy to wrap our finite brains around this infinite truth—but it is the truth! God wants a relationship with you, and he was willing to let his son die to get it. Ah, but Jesus was lifted and resurrected back to life again, defeating the devil, and now we have the precious opportunity to be called sons and daughters of God because of what

Jesus did! Once this awesome truth settles down into your soul, you will never be the same nor will you ever look at relationships the same way again. God is jealous for your attention, believe it or not, and once you give him that, you will become the kind of person who will be beneficial to whoever he brings you to, or you will become more beneficial to who you are already with. Bottom line: keep looking to Jesus because he is the only one who can give you what you need, not another person. God bless you, and I hope this chapter has helped.

God Blessed
the Broken Road

"And he that sat upon the throne said,
'Behold, I make all things new.'"

—Revelation 1:5a (KJV)

As I LOOK back over my life, I can plainly see the finger-prints of God. However, in those individual moments, it oftentimes felt like God was nowhere to be found. Winston Churchill rightly said, "The further back you can look, the further forward you will be able to see." With that in mind, I thank God that I am alive to look back over my past, not with regret anymore but with gratitude in that God let me live to see the other side of the fence in sobriety. So often

I've been really good at talking about the horrible times of addiction and homelessness and the near escapes from death, so I think it is also a good thing to reminisce over the blessings on the other side of the fence. Next to salvation, I'd have to say the greatest blessing of my life has been my wife, Johanna Cosby. Like I had said in one chapter that we met praying backstage, God definitely blessed the broken road that had led us to that point. By God's grace, she has allowed me many different times to share her story of brokenness when I speak to groups and how God used those broken pieces to weave together a beautiful tapestry if you will. I would like to dedicate a portion of this chapter to show how, like a phoenix, she rose from the ashes to lay hold of a new life that God had planned for her. Around the same time in 2005, when I was starting my journey back toward Christ, she too was dealing with a life situation that would have destroyed most of us. Her marriage had fallen apart under the strain of her and her first husband, losing their daughter to a tragic drowning, and now having to deal with the new norm of being a single mom not making much money and left with a bunch of bills she had to put her knuckles to the ground and get serious about life, or life would get serious for her and knock the wind out of her. There's something to be said about some single moms who deny the temptations to throw a pity party and, for the sake of their children, zero in on making life as normal as possible for them so that they do not grow up with the stigma of a mother and father who just couldn't get along. Johanna I tip my hat to you for not only doing that, but continuing to put others first even when they tell you to go first. You really do have a servant's heart in you. It was during this time that I was going through my furnace in prison, and she was going through the furnace of divorce. God was teaching me the skill of being content with just him, and at the same time, he was teaching her the skill of learning how to trust him when there seemed to be no way out. The funny thing is that I was almost right down the street from her during this time at Shelby County corrections, and she lived in Cordova, only about ten minutes away. Who knew that as I was praying in my cell for the woman God was preparing for me, she was almost right down the street! God has a strange sense of humor. Fast forward to the moment we were praying next to each other almost four and a half years later, we had both attempted to try dating with other people months before we had even met just to realize that we were pulling our arms away from the guiding hand of God to try something our way, just because of boredom and being alone. I remember the months following after I had met Johanna—and after many cups of coffee and conversation—I realized that we both had chosen to give up on looking for someone and when we had done that, it wasn't but a few months that we met each other! Again, if you want God to laugh, tell Him your plans.

On January 23, 2011, she threw me a surprise birthday party at her house and had gathered all of my family together. We had been dating about seven months or so by this point, and I have to be honest, there were a couple times that the old Danny tried to get in the way, and I tried to back out of the relationship a few times, only to find that as soon as I would leave her, I wanted to be back with her again. I thank God for a wonderful woman named Ephie Johnson, who was the choir director at Hope Church when I met Johanna. She had become great friends with me and Johanna, and also knew Johanna through some of her struggles. There was a week in particular I asked Johanna to "give me a week to think things through," that I didn't know if I really wanted to be in a relationship or not. I'm surprised she didn't kick me to the curb then, but she talked to Ephie, and Ephie said, "Girl, if he needs a week, give him a week. You're worth waiting for, and he's worth waiting for." It wasn't even a day later after Johanna said, "Sure, take a week and let me know," that I called her up, sobbing, telling her that I love her and believed that she was my soul mate. For all the guys reading this, I apologize for the mushiness, but if you are honest with yourself, you want the same thing!

Well, back to the surprise birthday party. Johanna and I had had conversations about marriage, and even look at some rings but with the thought of probably not getting married for several years from this time. Well, that Sunday the 23rd of January 2011, I left Hope Church after singing and flew out to Kay's jewelry in Collierville because the day before I had bought an engagement ring but knew in my heart it wasn't the one I wanted. I had my eyes on another one that was a few hundred dollars more, and I didn't want to spend the money, but I knew that was the one I wanted. So I shot up there, exchanged the rings, paid the money, and went to play racquetball with my dad at the Y.

After the game, I showed him the ring and told him what I was going to do because I figured she was going to have some kind of party with maybe my parents there, but I had no idea she was inviting everybody! After playing, my dad and I went outside on the roof of the YMCA downtown Memphis looked up to the sky, committed what I was about to do to the Lord, and then I said a prayer of sorts to her parents, Angie and John, who are with the Lord. I kid you not, as soon as I asked her father in prayer for permission to marry his daughter, a little circle opened up in the sky like it does sometimes around the sun, even if it was a cloudy day, and I had a feeling of peace that her daddy said, "You have my blessing, son." What was doubly amazing is Johanna told me once that she had an image of her daughter Emily, who passed away, running through a field of yellow flowers; and, ironically when I went back to my truck to leave the YMCA and head to her house, there was a little napkin on the ground near my door with yellow flowers on it, which looked like it had never been used! Call me crazy, but to this day I think Emily said, "I'm glad you're going to marry my momma." Well, once I got to her house and walked in, I was greeted by loud "surprise!" Everybody was there—friends and family, and I was personally happy because I wanted everyone to see me ask her to marry me. I didn't waste much time. I had only been there about ten minutes, and I gathered everyone in the living room. Johanna told me later that she thought I was simply going to pray over the food! Well, I thanked everyone for being there and then immediately reached into my pocket, turned toward her, walked toward her, hit my knees, and recited something my mom helped me come up with. It went a little something like this, "Johanna, I know you don't want one, and I know that you said you don't need one, but you deserve one, so with this ring, will you marry me?" I guess she was in total shock because, after about forty-five long seconds, she finally shook her head yes. I was relieved! We married on July 15th of that same year, and it was wonderful because just about everyone we knew at Hope Church pitched in to help us have a wonderful wedding from the food, to the music, to the preachers— even her wedding dress—were all gifts from people whom we love, and if you're reading this book and were a part of that, know that you played an awesome role in blessing two people who had almost given up on life until they found each other. Thank you so much! To this day, as I write this book, I thank God for blessing the broken roads in my life. I know many of you can relate and agree with me, and I know many of you reading this are in the middle of what appears to be a broken road with nowhere to go and no way out, and I want to encourage you in the name of Jesus right now, that if he can make a way for me he can, will, and wants to make a way for you! I know it seems like there's no way out, and no way that your situation could be blessed, but for me it was when I gave up and said, "Jesus, take the wheel," and I literally let go of it this time. This is when he drove my life into the city of blessings, and I pray that you will be able to do the same thing! Every day has not been roses, but I will tell you this much, that God did bless my broken road, and my good days definitely outweigh my bad.